# GREAT ILLUSTRATED CLASSICS

# THE WAR OF THE WORLDS

## H.G Wells

adapted by
Malvina G. Vogel

**Illustrations by Brendan Lynch**

BARONET BOOKS, New York, New York

# GREAT ILLUSTRATED CLASSICS

### edited by
### Malvina G. Vogel

Cover Copyright © MCMXCVII
Playmore Inc., Publishers and
Waldman Publishing Corp.,
New York, New York. All Rights Reserved

Interior Text and Art Copyright © MCMLXXXIII
Playmore Inc., Publishers and
Waldman Publishing Corp.,
New York, New York. All Rights Reserved

BARONET BOOKS is a registered trademark of Playmore Inc., Publishers
and Waldman Publishing Corp., New York, New York

No part of this book may be reproduced
or copied in any form without written
permission of the publisher.

Printed in the United States of America

# Contents

# About the Author

H.G. Wells was a famous English writer of novels, history and science books, and science-fiction stories. But the Herbert George Wells who was born in a London suburb in 1866 didn't appear destined for such fame. His father, a poor shopkeeper, could not afford a proper education for his son, so the boy was apprenticed to a cloth-maker, and later to a chemist.

But Wells was not content with this work, and by studying hard, he won a scholarship to the The Royal College of Science, where he studied biology. His training as a scientist and his love of writing led him to produce such imaginative science-fiction works as *The Time Machine, The Invisible Man, The First Men in the Moon,* and *The War of the Worlds.*

The inspiration for *The War of the Worlds* came one day when Wells and his brother Frank were strolling through the peaceful countryside in Surrey, south of London. They were discussing the invasion of the Australian island of Tasmania in the early 1800's by European settlers, who hunted down and killed most of the primitive people who lived there. To emphasize the reaction of these people, Frank said, "Suppose some beings from another planet were to drop out of the sky suddenly and begin taking over Surrey and then all of England!"

Wells was inspired by that "Suppose..." and went on to study the Surrey countryside, its towns and its people. From this, came the Martian invasion of Surrey in *The War of the Worlds*.

H.G. Wells died at the age of 80, in 1946, but of all of his scientific and historical works, it is for his science-fiction stories that he is best remembered by millions of readers today.

Unnoticed by Most Readers

# CHAPTER 1

## Mysterious Bursts of Flame

The little note in the London *Daily Telegraph* on the 13th of August, 1894, went almost unnoticed by most readers:

*Flaming Gas Bursts From Mars*
*Reports from the island of Java indicate the sighting of a mass of flaming hydrogen gas bursting out from the surface of Mars about midnight on the 12th. This flaming gas appeared to be moving with enormous speed towards Earth, but within fifteen minutes, it became invisible.*

I myself had missed the article, so I was completely ignorant of what would soon become one of the greatest dangers to the human race. And I might have stayed ignorant until it was too late had I not met my old friend Ogilvy, a well-known astronomer, while out for a stroll.

"I say there, Wells," he exclaimed upon seeing me, "what do you think of the news from Mars?"

"News?" I asked, puzzled. "What news could there be from a planet 40 million miles from here?"

"An exciting and unusual happening," cried Ogilvy. "A great light—a blaze almost—has burst from the surface of Mars."

I looked at him quizzically, not quite certain that I could share his excitement.

Guessing my thoughts, Ogilvy suggested, "Why not come up to my observatory tonight? We can study the heavens together."

"Why not?" I thought, so I agreed to go.

That night at midnight, I was taking my

Wells Meets His Old Friend, Ogilvy.

turn at the telescope when I saw a reddish flash around the edge of Mars. "Come quickly, Ogilvy!" I cried.

I never dreamed then that the flash was the launching of an accurately aimed missile from Mars, following the same path to Earth taken by the first one only 24 hours before. Yes, the Things they were sending to us were flying swiftly and steadily across 40 million miles to bring much death and destruction to Earth.

"Well, Ogilvy," I said, as he turned away from the telescope an hour later, "are the Martians signaling us?" In the darkness of the observatory, he couldn't see the mocking smile on my face.

"Ridiculous!" he cried. "It is probably some meteorites falling in a heavy shower on Mars, or perhaps a huge volcano exploding."

"But why do you doubt the existence of life on Mars?" I asked.

"The chances of any sort of human life there are a million to one," he replied. "Remember,

"Come Quickly, Ogilvy!"

man, Mars is 140 million miles from the sun, and the light and heat it gets is barely half of what we get on Earth. Human life could not survive, for Mars is getting colder and colder."

"But there is air and water on Mars," I argued. "Wouldn't that support life?"

"Perhaps . . . perhaps," he replied, deep in thought, "but surely not life as advanced as ours."

Little did I know that night that our planet was being watched closely by beings with greater intelligence than man, beings who were just as mortal as man, beings who had created instruments and weapons man has scarcely dreamed of, beings who watched Earth enviously, and slowly made their plans to leave their dying planet and take over their only hope for survival—a green, fertile planet crowded with what they considered inferior animals.

Other observers on Earth saw the flame burst forth from Mars that night, the night after, and again each night after that, for a

Watching Earth!

total of ten nights. Why the shots stopped after the tenth night, no one on Earth attempted to explain.

Meanwhile, the missiles the Martians had fired at us sped earthward at many miles a second, nearer and nearer. But even with this death and destruction hanging over us, men went about their daily activities, peaceful and safe, giving only an occasional glance at the bright dot of light in the heavens called Mars.

Martian Missiles Speed Earthward.

Ogilvy Sees the Shooting Star.

# CHAPTER 2

## The Landing of the Martians

Then came the night of the first falling star—a line of flame high in the sky, traveling with a hissing sound and leaving a greenish streak behind it. Most observers thought that another meteorite had fallen—an event of such little importance that no one took the trouble to look for it the night it fell.

But Ogilvy had seen the shooting star and set out along the common—a stretch of open land—between the towns of Horsell, Chobham, and Woking to find it. And find it he did, near the sand pits.

An enormous hole had been made by the impact of the Thing, and the sand and gravel had been flung violently in every direction, forming high mounds visible a mile away. The small evergreen bushes, known as heather, were on fire all around the hole, and the Thing itself lay almost entirely buried in the sand.

As Ogilvy reached the edge of the hole, he looked down and saw one section of the Thing partly uncovered. It seemed to be a huge cylinder about 90 feet in diameter, and was caked over by a thick gray crust. Since it was still extremely hot from its flight, Ogilvy was unable to get close enough to examine it.

As he stood on the edge of the pit at sunrise, the sounds of faint movements came from inside the cylinder. "An unequal cooling of the surface," muttered Ogilvy, never dreaming that the Thing might be hollow!

Suddenly, some of the grayish crust covering the meteorite began falling off the uncovered end of the cylinder. Ogilvy was disturbed.

The Thing!

"Why is it falling only from the end of the cylinder?" he asked himself. "If the meteorite is cooling, the crust should be falling from the whole body."

And then he saw the circular top slowly...slowly...slowly rotating on its body, then give a sudden jerk an inch or two outward.

"Good Heavens!" he cried. "The cylinder is hollow, with an end that screws out! Something or someone inside is unscrewing the top. They must be roasting to death and trying to escape! But where did they come fr—?" And then the realization hit him. "That flash on Mars!" he exclaimed. "Oh, that poor creature trapped inside! I must free him!"

And forgetting the heat, Ogilvy ran down the embankment of the sand pit to try to help turn the cylinder. But the radiation that the Thing gave off stopped him before he could burn his hands. He froze for a moment, then scrambled out of the pit and set off running wildly into Woking to get help.

Ogilvy Rushes To Help.

The first few people he approached at 6 o'clock that morning thought him a raving lunatic and hurried on their way. Finding himself at the home of Henderson, the London newspaperman, and seeing him in the garden, Ogilvy ran up to him.

"Henderson," he shouted, "did you see that shooting star last night? It's out on Horsell Common."

"Good Lord!" cried Henderson. "A fallen meteorite—that would make a good story!"

"But it's more than a meteorite," explained Ogilvy. "It's a cylinder—a hollow cylinder—and there's something inside!"

Henderson froze with his spade in his hand. "What did you say?" he gasped.

Ogilvy told him all that he had seen. When he was done, Henderson dropped the spade, and the two men ran off down the road toward Horsell Common.

The cylinder was still lying in the same position, but the sounds inside had ceased.

Ogilvy and Henderson rapped on the crusty

Teling Henderson About the Shooting Star

cylinder with sticks, but got no response.

"They've either fainted, or they're dead!" whispered Ogilvy.

"No! No!" shouted Henderson. "We must find them alive!" Then rapping again with his stick, Henderson called to the opening, "Hold on in there, whoever you are. We'll get you out. We'll go for help."

Once back in Woking, Henderson and Ogilvy ran up and down the streets in the bright sunlight, shouting the news to shop-folks who were taking down their shutters and to people opening their bedroom windows.

Henderson went to the railway station and telegraphed the news to London.

I heard the news less than an hour later from the lips of the young boy who delivered my newspaper from town.

"And," the boy added, "boys and men from Woking have already gone out to the sand pits to see the dead men from Mars."

I was startled, but I lost no time in going out to the sand pits myself.

Rapping on the Cylinder with Sticks

Since the papers had already come out with headlines shouting, "A Message from Mars!" hundreds of people were crowded around the pit, their horses, carts, carriages, and bicycles standing by.

I made my way to the edge of the pit and saw half a dozen men working with spades and pickaxes below. There was Ogilvy, the newspaperman Henderson, and the Royal Astronomer, Stent.

Stent was standing on the cylinder, his face steaming with perspiration, as he gave directions to the workmen who were busy uncovering much of the cylinder.

"Halloa there, Wells," called Ogilvy when he spied me at the edge of the crowd. "We've been hearing faint movements inside, but my workmen can't get a grip on the top to unscrew it. We shall just have to wait until it opens by itself."

Feeling somewhat disappointed, I moved away through the crowd, when suddenly from the edge of the pit, I heard loud voices and felt

Ogilvy Greets Wells.

the crowd pushing back.

"It's a-movin'," shouted a boy as he ran by me. "It's a-screwin' and a-screwin' out. I don't like it one bit. I'm goin' home, I am."

When I reached the edge, I heard a peculiar humming coming from the Thing, and I saw the end of the cylinder being unscrewed . . . automatically from within!

Just then, someone in the crowd pushed against me, and as I turned to retain my balance and keep from falling into the pit, I heard a clang. I turned quickly back to the pit to find that the lid had fallen out completely, and now lay in the gravel. Ogilvy and his men were scampering out of the pit.

I guess I expected to see a man come out from the Thing—not exactly a man like me, but a man of some sort nevertheless. As I gazed into the shadows, I saw some gray wavy movements, one above the other, and then two luminous circles—like eyes. Then something resembling a little gray snake, about as thick as a cane, coiled up out of the middle of the

The Lid Falls Out—By Itself!

form and wriggled and writhed its way through the air. First one, then another and another.

I drew back from the edge of the pit, staring, still unable to tear my eyes away from the many tentacles that were now projecting from this grayish mass. Horror showed on every face around me as most of the people turned and ran.

I stood petrified, staring, as a big grayish rounded bulk about the size of a bear rose out of the cylinder. As the last rays of the sun hit it, it glistened like wet leather.

Two large, dark-colored eyes stared back at me, and the surface above them was flat, with no hint of a ridge where eyebrows usually grew. The mass that surrounded those eyes was round—almost like a face. Below the eyes was a strange V-shaped mouth, with its pointed upper lip quivering and saliva dripping from it as the creature trembled and panted, almost as if in a convulsion. There was no chin beneath the wedgelike lower lip.

A Rounded Bulk Rises out of the Cylinder.

# THE WAR OF THE WORLDS

As one of its thin tentacles gripped the edge of the cylinder and another swayed in the air, the monster suddenly toppled over the rim of the cylinder and fell into the pit. It's fall sounded like a loud leathery thud. The creature gave a strange cry, and immediately another of them appeared at the opening of the cylinder.

I turned and ran wildly towards a group of trees, stumbling as I ran, for I could not tear my eyes from the pit. The field around the pit was still dotted with people standing, like myself, staring at these creatures in fascination and terror. My body was paralyzed with fear, but my brain was sparked with curiosity about these creatures and the cylinder in which they had come to Earth from Mars.

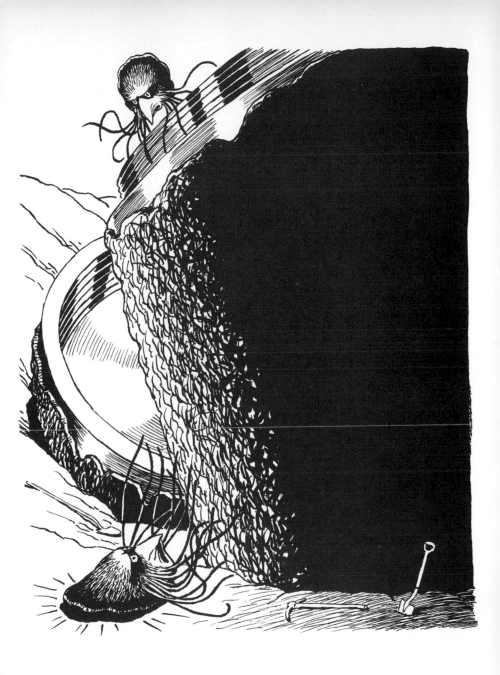

Another Creature Appears.

A Rod Rises Above the Pit.

# CHAPTER 3

## The Heat-Ray

I didn't dare go back towards the pit, but I longed to gaze into it. I began walking in a big curve, seeking some higher ground from which I could see into the pit, but not be seen by the Martians.

Once, a leash of black tentacles, like the arms of an octopus, reached above the pit, then immediately disappeared. Soon afterwards, a thin rod appeared, rising joint by joint. At the tip of the rod was a disc that spun around in a wobbling motion. What could it be?

By now, most of the people on the common had gathered in two groups on opposite sides of the pit. I stationed myself on a small hill, slightly higher than the crowds of people, but for a long while, as the sun set and afterward, nothing further happened. This gave the crowd new confidence, and small groups of people began to move towards the pit.

At this moment, Ogilvy, Stent, and Henderson came out from behind a tree and, waving a white flag, headed for the pit.

"What do you plan to do?" I called to Ogilvy.

"We've had a conference," he explained, "and we've decided that the Martians are obviously intelligent creatures even though their bodies are monstrous. So we are going to show them that we, too, are intelligent."

Before I had a chance to comment on Ogilvy's explanation, a flash of light came out of the pit and three long, powerful puffs of green flame rose up one after the other into the air, followed by a faint hissing sound. The hissing changed to a loud humming noise.

Waving a White Flag

The humming was revealed as coming from something humped, or domed-shaped, as it slowly rose out of the pit. Flickers of white flame leaped out from it and towards the men with the white flag. In an instant, each man turned to fire, staggered, and fell!

I stood staring, hardly realizing that this noiseless, blinding flame brought death as it leaped from man to man in this group and then continued on from man to woman to child around the common. It brought fiery destruction as well, as it leaped swiftly from trees to bushes to distant wooden buildings.

Just as the white flame was leaping toward the hill on which I was standing, the hissing and humming ceased, and the black dome-like object sank slowly out of sight into the pit.

All this had happened so swiftly that I stood motionless, dumfounded and dazzled by the flashes of light. If that flame, or Heat-Ray, as I called it, had made a full circle, it would have caught me in its path. But it passed me by, thus sparing my life.

The White Flame!

I gazed at the spot where the little group with the white flag had stood only minutes before. This little group no longer existed. The people around them had either fled with the first burst of flame or had been protected by high sand hills as the Heat-Ray passed over their heads. But as the trees above them caught fire, sparks and burning twigs fell on them. Hats and dresses caught fire. Shrieks and shouts filled the air as men, women and children pushed at those in their way to reach the road to Woking, crushing and trampling each other in the darkness.

I suddenly realized I was alone on this dark common, helpless and unprotected. With a panic and terror I had never before known, I turned and ran stumbling through the heather, crashing blindly into trees and passing more than forty bodies, burned and destroyed beyond recognition. I ran until I could go no farther. Then I staggered and fell by the roadside. How long I lay there I do not know.

When I finally sat up, I began to wonder if

Fleeing the Heat-Ray

I—a decent, ordinary citizen—had dreamed everything. I got up unsteadily and staggered as if I were drunk. Everything around me— the night, my home on Maybury Hill ahead, a train passing in the distance—everything was so serene, so normal, so familiar. But behind me...

Reaching Maybury, I spied two men and a woman talking at the gate of one house in a row of pretty little houses.

"What news is there from the common?" I gasped weakly.

"Ain't yer just been there?" asked one of the men, seeing the direction from which I had come.

"People are actin' silly about the common," said the woman. "What's it all about?"

"Haven't you heard about the creatures from Mars?" I asked, surprised.

"Quite enough, thanks," said the woman with a laugh. The men joined her laughter.

"But the ra...." I began. "And Ogilvy and

Wells Asks For News.

Henderson and Stent...." I tried again. But I could not finish my sentences.

The two men and the woman laughed again. I felt foolish and angry.

"You'll hear more yet," I cried and turned away from them to head toward my house.

My appearance—so haggard and dirty—startled my wife, but she led me into the dining room, and poured me some wine.

I finally gathered up enough energy to tell her what I had seen. Seeing fear spread over her face, I tried to reassure her. "Do not become alarmed, my dear. These creatures are the most sluggish things ever to crawl. They will probably keep control of the pit and kill people who come near it, but they cannot get out."

"But they might," she said with concern, "and they might come here."

I poured some wine for her and tried again to reassure her. "But they can scarcely move. Ogilvy explained to me how the force of gravity on earth is three times stronger than on

Telling His Wife the News

Mars. Therefore, a Martian would weigh three times more on earth than on Mars, although his strength would be the same. Don't you see, my dear, his own body would be a lead weight to him."

My wife was still pale with fear. "But why have they killed so many already?"

"They are quite possibly mad with terror," I said reassuringly. "It was a foolish act, but perhaps they came to Earth not really expecting to find any living things. And now, my dear, let us have a pleasant dinner and leave the Martians for the government and the police to handle."

I did not know it, but that was the last civilized dinner I was to eat for many strange and terrible days.

The Last Civilized Dinner!

Watching the Heath Burn

# CHAPTER 4

## The Second Cylinder Falls

Throughout England that Friday evening, people were having dinner, working men tending to their gardens at the end of their daily chores, children were being put to bed, young couples were wandering the lanes, and students were sitting over their books. The daily routine of working, eating, drinking, and sleeping went on as it had for years—as though no planet Mars existed in the sky.

But in the houses facing the commons in the villages of Woking, Horsell, and Chobham, people stayed awake watching the heath burn from the Martians' Heat-Ray.

Now and again the Heat-Ray swept the common, catching a few adventurous souls who had gone out in the darkness to see the Martians. But blackened bodies, lying twisted in death, were all that remained of them.

All night long the Martians were hammering and stirring, sleepless and untiring, at work on the machine that would bring more death and destruction. Now and again a puff of greenish-white smoke whirled out from the cylinder up to the sky.

About eleven o'clock columns of soldiers came through Horsell and Chobham, and formed a cordon around the edge of the common.

A few seconds after midnight, a group of people on Chertsey Road outside of Woking saw a star fall from the sky into the pine woods to the northwest. The star had a greenish color, and caused a silent, but bright flash of light. This was the second cylinder!

The Second Cylinder Falls.

The Milkman Brings News.

# CHAPTER 5

## Fighting Begins

Saturday was a day of suspense. I had slept very little, rose early, and went out into my garden to look towards the common.

The milkman pulled up in his wagon and greeted me.

"Is there any news?" I asked.

"Yes, sir. During the night our troops surrounded the Martians. We're expecting some large guns any time. But the orders are not to kill them, if it can possibly be avoided. They also say that another of those blessed things has fallen in the woods." And he pointed towards a haze of smoke in the distance.

I decided to walk down towards the common after breakfast, but soldiers had the road blocked off, so I returned home.

All during that hot, dull day, the Martians didn't show an inch of themselves. They were obviously busy in the pit, for there was a continuous hammering and a continuous stream of smoke.

About three o'clock, I heard the thud of a gun from the direction of Chertsey. I learned that the smouldering pine woods into which the second cylinder had fallen was being shelled, in the hopes of destroying the object before it opened.

At six in the evening as I was sitting with my wife in the garden having tea, I heard a muffled explosion coming from the common, followed by a gust of rifle shots. Close on the heels of that came a violent rattling crash so close to us that it shook the very ground beneath us. I looked up and saw the tops of trees

Soldiers Block the Road.

around the Maybury Hill school burst into smokey red flames and the tower of the little church beside it slide down into ruin. Then one of the chimneys in my house cracked as if a shot had hit it, and pieces of it came clattering down into the flower bed below my study window. I suddenly realized that the top of Maybury Hill, where we lived, must be within range of the Martians' Heat-Ray!

"We cannot stay here," I cried as I gripped my wife's arm and ran her out into the road.

"But where can we go?" she cried in terror.

"Leatherhead!" I shouted above the noise of new firing from the common. "To your cousins in Leatherhead. I'll go down the hill immediately and rent a horse and cart."

While my wife and our servant rushed into the house to pack a few valuables, I went for the cart.

As I drove back up Maybury Hill, I saw a group of soldiers enter the village, running from house to house warning people to leave.

I packed my wife, our servant, and their

The Heat-Ray Hits Wells's Chimney.

valuables into the cart, then jumped up into the driver's seat. A whirl of black smoke covered the road on our side of Maybury Hill, but in moments we were heading down the other side of the hill, away from the smoke and noise and fire.

We made the 20-mile trip to Leatherhead safely, and I left my silent, terrified wife in her cousins' care. I tried to reassure her that I would be safe upon my return to Maybury. "After all," I told her, "those Martians are too heavy to get out of the pit."

My wife would have liked me to stay at Leatherhead with her, but I had to return the horse and cart I rented. In my heart I was not sorry that I had to return to Maybury. I had been very excited all day—almost a war, fever—and I wanted to be there when the Martians were destroyed.

It was nearly eleven o'clock when I left Leatherhead, and I had no way of knowing how the evening's fighting had been going.

As I came down one hill and Maybury came

Heading Away from the Fire

into view in front of me, a horrible glare of green fire lit the field to my left. Suddenly, crashing into that field was...the third falling star!

I had little time to do more than glance quickly, for at that moment, a blinding flash of lightning, followed by a bursting clap of thunder, startled my horse. He bolted and took off swiftly down the hill. I tried to keep my eyes on the road though a blinding rain beat against my face.

Suddenly my attention was diverted by something moving rapidly down Maybury Hill. A flash of lightning, creating an instant of daylight, revealed this Thing—clear and sharp and bright!

It was a monstrous metal Thing—a walking engine on three legs, taller than most houses. It was walking over young pine trees in its path and smashing them aside, its metal clattering noisily along with the thunder.

Another flash! And it appeared even clearer. It seemed to move by tilting over on one metal

A Walking Engine!

leg while two were raised in the air. With this noisy motion, it was able to gain nearly 300 feet with each step!

Suddenly the trees in the pine wood ahead of me parted, and a second huge Thing appeared, rushing, as it seemed, headlong towards me. And my horse was galloping right towards it! At the sight of this second monster, I lost my nerve completely. I pulled the reins so far to the right that the tug turned over the horse and I was flung out of the cart.

I landed in a shallow pond and poked my head above the edge just far enough to be able to see. The horse lay dead in the road with a broken neck, poor brute! And one wheel on the overturned cart was still spinning slowly. I held my breath as the monstrous Thing went striding by me.

From where I lay hidden I was able to see the Thing up close. I soon realized that this was no mere automatic machine. A machine—yes, for it was metal. Atop its three tall legs was a kind of hood—a dome-like structure—

The Thing Rushes Towards Wells!

which seemed to rotate from side to side, looking very much like a head looking around, as it chose the path to follow.

From this dome, long flexible glittering tentacles—like arms—reached out, swinging and rattling around its strange body. One of these tentacles was carrying a young pine tree in its grip.

As the monster passed me, heading uphill, a deafening howl that sounded like "Aloo! Aloo!" came from it. During the flashes of lightning, I saw a huge white metal basket hanging behind its body and puffs of green smoke squirting from the joints of its legs.

In a minute the Thing joined his companion, and the two of them headed to the left, towards the green smoke. Reaching a field about a half-mile away, they stooped over the third of the ten cylinders they had fired at us.

I lay in the pond in the darkness, soaked with the rain above and the pond water below. It was some time before I could get over my astonishment and struggle up the bank to a drier

Tentacles Uproot a Pine Tree.

spot . . . or even think at all about the danger I was in. I stumbled into a ditch and crawled along it.

The rain was still pouring down in torrents, and my wet and shivering body was driven by one thought—to reach my own warm, dry house on Maybury Hill.

I soon left the ditch and followed a fence along the road, dragging myself along its rails. Near the top I stumbled upon something soft. The light flashed, and I saw at my feet a pile of black cloth and a pair of boots. I stood there waiting for the next flash and when it came, I saw that the pile was a man with his head bent under his body. He lay crumpled up close to the fence as he had been flung violently against it. I stooped and turned him over to feel for his heartbeat. He was quite dead. His neck had been broken.

I stepped over him and pushed on up the hill, stumbling through the darkened village. Nothing was burning, but a reddish smoke still rose from the common.

Stumbling upon Something Soft

Reaching my house, I let myself in and locked and bolted the door behind me. I collapsed at the foot of the staircase, shivering violently as my thoughts returned to those metallic monsters and to the dead body smashed against the fence.

I don't know how long I sat there, dazed and cold and wet, but when my eye caught the pools of water forming about me on the carpet, I got up and made my way into the dining room for a drink of whiskey.

Once I had changed into dry clothes, I went upstairs to my study. From the window I could look out on the common around the sand pit. Everything in that direction was lit by a vivid red glare. Busily moving to and fro across the light were the huge grotesque black shapes of the mechanical monsters. But with two miles separating us, I could not make out what they were doing.

As my eyes traveled down the hill along the Maybury Road toward Woking station, I saw the countryside burning and several houses

Dazed and Cold and Wet!

and streets around the station in growing ruins. Along the tracks I saw a wrecked train with its engine smashed and burning and its cars still on the rails.

This fiery chaos had once been my quiet, peaceful little world. I don't think I was quite certain exactly what had happened in the last seven hours, but I was beginning to guess the relationship between the mechanical monsters and the strange shapes I had seen leaving the cylinders.

Seating myself in my desk chair turned toward the window, I watched these three-legged metallic monsters busy at work. "What can they be?" I asked myself. "Intelligent mechanisms?... Impossible! Perhaps a Martian is sitting inside each monster, ruling and directing it, just as a man's brain sits and rules his body."

Just then, I heard a noise at my garden fence. I rose quickly and looked down. A man in a soldier's uniform was climbing over the fence.

"What Can They Be?"

"Halloa!" I said in an eager whisper.

He hesitated, then came across the lawn and called up, also in a whisper, "Who's there?"

"Are you looking for a place to hide?" I asked.

"Yes, yes."

"Come into the house, then," I said, and I went downstairs to unbolt the door.

Once the man was inside, I locked the door again. "What has happened?" I asked.

"What hasn't!" he replied, throwing his hands up in despair. "They wiped us out—simply wiped us out." With that, he sat down at the dining room table, put his head on his arms, and began to weep like a child.

I let him cry for a while as I stood beside him. When he seemed a little calmer, I asked, "Who are you, man, and where have you come from?"

"An artillery man, sir," he said brokenly. "We got called into action only at seven this evening when reports came in that the Martians on Horsell common were crawling slowly

"They Wiped Us Out."

towards their second cylinder under cover of a metal shield. Later, this shield staggered up on three legs and became a Fighting-Machine."

"Yes," I replied, "I saw that Fighting-Machine."

"Anyway, sir, my orders were to fire on the sand pit. As I approached on my horse, the beast caught his leg in a rabbit hole and threw me into a ditch. At that very moment, the gun I was to command and its ammunition exploded behind me, and I suddenly found myself under a pile of burned dead men and dead horses."

"My God!" I cried. "And you lived to tell it!"

"I lay still, sir," he continued, "scared out of my wits. We had been wiped out! And the smell—good God! Like burned meat! I was half-buried under a dead horse, but as I raised my head to peep out, I saw our foot soldiers— God rest their souls!—rush the pit.

"The monster rose to its feet—a hundred feet high, I'd swear, sir—and began to walk

"Ammunition Exploded Behind Me."

across the common on its three legs. That hood on top was turning back and forth just like the head of a human being, while a kind of arm carried a strange-looking metal box that gave off green flashes. Suddenly that box shot out a ray of light that destroyed every soldier, every tree, and every bush on the common.

"The Heat-Ray!" I cried.

"But the monster didn't stop with the common," cried the soldier. "It went right on to Woking station and left it in fiery ruins. Very few people were alive, and those who were, were burned and scalded. I saw the Thing chase a man, pick him up in one of its steely tentacles, and knock his head against the trunk of a tree. It was ghastly!"

"When you finally freed yourself from under the horse, where did you go?" I asked.

"I started towards Maybury here, hoping to continue on to London."

"Then good Lord, man, you must be hungry and thirsty," I cried.

"Yes, sir," he replied weakly.

"That Box Shot Out a Ray of Light."

I found some mutton and bread, and we sat down to eat.

We did not light a lamp for fear of attracting the Martians. As the morning light grew from the East, we saw three of the Fighting-Machines standing around the pit, their hoods rotating back and forth, back and forth, as if they were looking over the valley of ashes and ruins they had created.

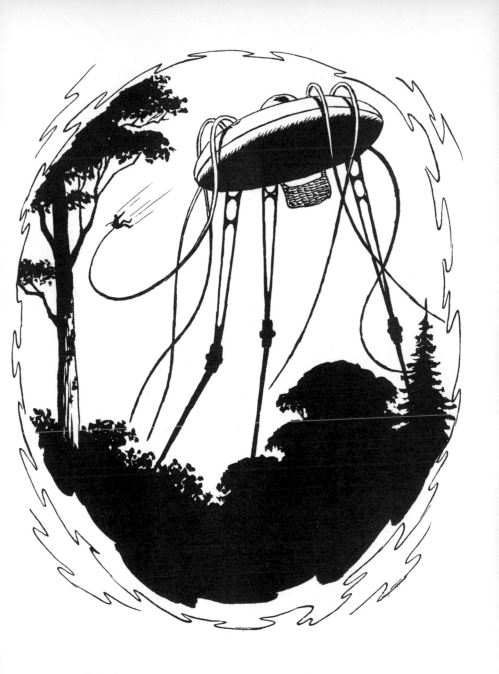

Picking Up a Man in Its Tentacles

Preparing to Travel

# CHAPTER 6

## A Battle in the Thames

As the dawn grew brighter, the artilleryman and I both agreed that the house was too dangerous a place to stay in. He wanted to rejoin the men of his battery who had not been on the common, and I wanted to return to my wife in Leatherhead and take her out of the country. However, between us and Leatherhead lay the third cylinder, with the giant Things guarding it.

We decided to travel part of the way together. But first, the artilleryman made me ransack the house for a canteen, which we filled with whiskey, and we both lined our pockets with biscuits and slices of meat.

We crept out of the house and ran as quickly as we could down the road, passing groups of charred bodies struck dead by the Heat-Ray. Alongside them were valuables such as clocks, silver spoons, and cash boxes, which these people had dropped as they tried to flee.

There was not a breath of wind that morning, and all the houses we passed were deserted. We saw not a living soul.

We reached the village of Byfleet safely. We were beyond the reach of the Heat-Ray, but the village was in chaos. People were packing their belongings, and scores of soldiers were helping them load wagons, carriages, carts, and anything they could find.

One old man was loading a huge box with dozens of orchids in flowerpots, while arguing with the corporal who was trying to persuade him to leave them behind.

"Do you know what's over there?" I cried,

Soldiers Help People Load Wagons.

running up to the old man and pointing beyond the pine forest toward Woking.

"Eh?" he said, holding an orchid pot in his arms. "I was explainin' these is vallyble."

"Death is over there!" I shouted. "Death is coming!" And I turned and left him staring quizzically at the trees.

The artilleryman and I made our way to the railway station which was swarming with people pushing, shoving, and struggling to be first on the trains which never came.

Leaving Byfleet, we made our way to the Thames River at Weybridge. Here, too, excited, noisy crowds of fugitives were trying to crowd into the ferryboats which crossed the river at this point.

People came from all directions, carrying household goods which they wanted to keep from the Martians who, they believed to be simply other human beings who might attack and rob their town. One husband and wife were carrying an outhouse door between them, with some of their household goods piled on it.

Fugitives Load Boats.

Suddenly a distant muffled thud—the sound of a gun—broke through the air.

"What's that?" cried the people near us. Everyone froze as they realized that the guns hidden in the thick woods around us were beginning to fight.

"The sojers'll stop 'em," said a woman beside me, but her face showed doubt.

Then a puff of smoke rose into the air up river, and the ground shook with a heavy explosion. Windows in nearby houses smashed in every direction.

"Here they are!" shouted a man as he dropped his suitcases. "Yonder!"

I quickly looked where he was pointing, and there, far away over the trees, appeared four of the Martian Fighting-Machines, striding quickly towards the river. Then a fifth joined them, holding a boxlike case high in the air. It was the ghastly, terrible Heat-Ray!

At the sight of these strange, swift, and terrible creatures, the crowd at the water's edge seemed to be horror-struck for a moment. No

Five Fighting-Machines Appear.

one screamed; no one shouted—there was only silence.... Then panic broke out. Even with the rush of people all around me, I was still able to think clearly.

"Get underwater!" I shouted, turning in all directions as I rushed down the beach, the artilleryman at my side. Some people followed me; others scattered into town.

The stones under my feet in the river were muddy and slippery, and the water, barely waist deep. But with one Martian Fighting-Machine towering overhead only a hundred yards away, I dove under the water. People around me were doing the same, while others leaped from boats to escape.

But the Martian took no more notice of the people running about than a man would of a nest of ants that his foot had kicked.

Half-choking, I raised my head above the water. The Fighting-Machine was at the bank of the river, starting to wade across, its Heat-Ray raised. As it reached the opposite bank, on the Shepperton side of the river, a battery of

"Get Underwater!"

six guns, which had been hidden in the woods outside the village, began firing.

The monster was raising its Heat-Ray as the first shell exploded a few feet above its hood. Two other shells burst in the air near its body, then a fourth exploded clean in its face.

Its hood flashed and whirled apart, bursting with fragments of red flesh and glittering metal.

"A hit!" I screamed.

"Hit! Hit!" shouted the people in the water around me.

The headless monster reeled like a drunken giant, but did not fall. It recovered its balance and lunged swiftly into Shepperton. The living creature—the Martian inside the hood—had been killed, and the Fighting-Machine was now simply a metal giant, driving wildly and out of control towards the town. It smashed into the church tower, reeled, and battered down buildings.

After several minutes, it finally collapsed with a tremendous explosion of water, steam,

"Hit! Hit!"

mud, and metal into the river upstream. Its gigantic limbs churned the water and flung splashes of foam and mud into the air. Its tentacles swayed like human arms struggling for life amid the waves.

As the Heat-Ray hit the water, it flashed into steam, and moments later a scalding hot wave came sweeping around the bend in the river.

Only the frantic shouts of the artilleryman near me in the water could tear my gaze from this death struggle. "Look, man, look!" he cried. "The others!"

There, on the river bank, advancing with gigantic strides, were the other Fighting-Machines. The Shepperton guns fired again, but with no success.

I immediately ducked underwater and moved towards shore. The water raged about me, getting hotter from the Heat-Ray's steam every moment.

I raised my head for a breath, and through the steam rising from the river I saw the

Struggling for Life Amid the Waves

colossal figures. They had passed by me, and two were stooping over the steaming ruins of their comrade.

The noises above water were deafening—the clanging of the Martians, the crash of falling houses, the thud of trees flashing into flame, and the crackling and roaring of fire. The Heat-Ray went back and forth across Weybridge on one side of the river.

For a moment I stood there, chest-high in near-boiling water, with no hope of escaping. People nearer the bank scrambled out of the water through the reeds, like little frogs hurrying through grass.

Suddenly the white flashes of the Heat-Ray came leaping towards me. Houses on shore caved in and burst into flames. Then the Ray flickered along the footpath which ran by the river, destroying people who ran this way and that. It came down to the water no more than fifty yards from where I stood and swept across to the Shepperton side. The water in its path rose in a boiling crest of steam.

Trying To Help Their Comrade

I turned toward shore, but not before a huge wave, almost at the boiling point, rushed upon me. I screamed aloud and, scalded, half-blind, and in agony, I staggered toward shore. Here, I fell helplessly upon gravely sand. I was in full view of the Martians . . . and expected nothing but death!

I dimly remember the foot of one Martian driving into the loose ground no more than a few feet from my head and lifting again. Through the smoke, I could make out four Martians carrying the remains of their comrade between them across the river and through a meadow beyond.

Very slowly, I realized that by a mistake I had escaped!

A Boiling Wave Rushes upon Wells.

Wells Finds an Abandoned Boat.

# CHAPTER 7

## The Curate

Seeing no sign of the artilleryman, I left the flaming wreckage of Weybridge and Shepperton behind me and started off along the river toward London.

An abandoned boat drifting downstream caught my attention through the steam that was still rising from the river. I threw off my shirt and shoes and jumped into the water to make my way to the boat. There were no oars inside, and I had to use my scalded, blistering hands to paddle.

"At last!" I thought. "By following the river, I have a better chance to escape if these giant Martians return."

Along both banks were deserted villages. Those houses which faced the river were blazing with flames in the heat of the afternoon.

I drifted for several hours, too weary and too much in pain to paddle. The sun scorched my bare back. Every so often my fears would get to me, and I would start paddling furiously. By about five o'clock, my fever and faintness overcame my fears, and I landed the boat just before the village of Walton.

After resting awhile amid the tall grass on the bank, I got up and began to walk, talking to myself, but not remembering what I was saying. When thirst took hold of me, I sat down to rest beneath a hedge and probably dozed.

When I opened my eyes, the sun was beginning to set. I became aware of a seated figure before me, staring at a faint flickering in the sky. I sat up quickly and asked, "Have you any water? I need a drink desperately."

Resting on the River Bank

He shook his head and said, "You have been asking for water for the last hour."

For a moment, we sat staring at each other silently. I must have been a strange sight— naked, except for my water-soaked trousers and socks, my skin scalded and blackened by smoke. He was dressed as a man of the church, but his blankly staring eyes made me doubt his strength and courage.

"Why has God permitted these things to happen?" he asked nervously. "What sins have we committed? I had just finished conducting morning services and had gone for a walk when suddenly—fire, earthquake, death! Everything gone—my church, the Sunday school—gone! Everything destroyed! Swept out of existence!"

From the wild stare in his eyes, I began to doubt his sanity. And the more he raved and ranted and repeated his questions to God, the more convinced I became.

"You must keep your head," I said quietly. "There is still hope."

The Man of the Church Raves and Rants.

"There is no hope!" he cried. "This is the beginning of the end!"

I struggled to my feet and laid my hand on his shoulder. "Be a man!" I said. "Earthquakes and floods, wars and volcanoes have destroyed men before, but there is hope."

"Can we escape?" he asked suddenly. "They seem indestructible—those terrible creatures."

"They are not indestructible," I explained. "One of them was killed not three hours ago. But they will come this way again and head for London. Let us be on our way."

"There Is Hope."

Police at Waterloo Station

# CHAPTER 8

## News Reaches London

My younger brother, Frank, a medical student, was studying for his exams in London when the Martians landed at Woking. When he learned of the cylinder in the afternoon newspapers on Saturday, he saw no cause for alarm, for he knew that the sand pit was a good two mines from my house. Still, he planned to come down to Maybury on Sunday to see the Things before they were killed.

But when he reached London's Waterloo Station on Sunday, he found police clearing people out to make room for troops and supplies heading for Woking. Newspaper boys, carrying their still-wet papers, converged on the street outside the station shouting, "Dreadful catastrophe! Fighting at Weybridge! Thousands killed!"

Then, and only then, did Frank realize the full power and terror of these monsters!

Fugitives from the battle area had already begun to enter London, their furniture, bundles, and boxes loaded onto carts and hay wagons. The faces of these people were tired and drawn, and their appearance was a great contrast to the Londoners on the street, dressed in their fashionable Sunday best.

Some of the fugitives were exchanging news with the people on the street.

"Saw the Martians myself," explained one dirty, ragged man. "Boilers on stilts, I tell you, striding along like a man."

Frank stopped several of these people to ask about me, but the only news he got was from

"Dreadful Catastrophe!"

a man who told him that Woking had been completely destroyed the previous night.

Although he was anxious about my safety, Frank decided to return home to await further news. It was during the early hours of Monday morning that he was awakened by the loud rapping of door knockers.

From his attic room he looked down to see policemen hammering at doors and shouting, "The Martians are coming!" Church bells were trying to awaken every Londoner as well. Carriages, cabs, and every kind of vehicle came flying by, heading for the train stations which led northward out of London.

Frank hurriedly began to dress, running to the window with each piece of clothing, in order not to miss any of the growing excitement.

Soon, men were selling unusually early morning newspapers, shouting in the streets, "London in danger of suffocation! Martians advancing! Fearful massacres in the Thames valley!"

Frank Dresses Quickly.

# THE WAR OF THE WORLDS

Unable to learn from his window what was happening, Frank ran down into the street just as the sky showed touches of dawn.

Crowds of people on foot and in vehicles grew more numerous every moment. "Black smoke!" they cried again and again.

Frank bought a newspaper from a seller who was part of the fleeing crowd. A report from the commander-in-chief of the army said:

*"The Martians shot out rockets which spread huge clouds of poisonous black smoke. This smoke has smothered our gun batteries along the route to London, destroyed everything on the way. It is impossible to stop the Martians. There is no escaping the black smoke, except to flee instantly."*

This was all, but it was enough to throw a city of six million people into a panic.

When Frank realized the full meaning of all those things, he returned quickly to his room, took all the money he had, and went back out into the streets.

Advancing Towards London

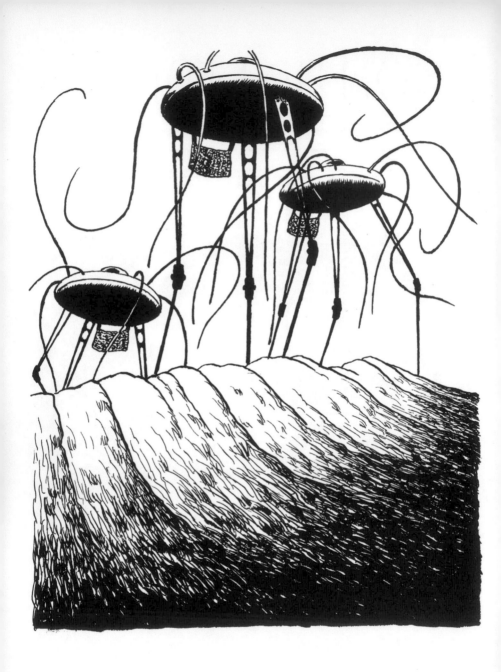

A City in Panic!

# CHAPTER 9

## The Attack of the Black Smoke

I later learned that on Sunday morning, while I had been sitting talking to the curate under the hedge and while Frank had been out on the street by Waterloo Station, the Martians had started preparing for another attack.

Three of the Fighting-Machines had come out of the pit about 8 o'clock on Sunday morning and started advancing slowly in a line, a mile and a half apart, northward towards London. They "spoke" to each other by means of assorted sirenlike howls.

The gunners defending the village of Ripley in the Martians' path were new artillery volunteers who should never have been placed in such a strategic position. They fired one wild, premature volley, then ran off. One Martian, without using his Heat-Ray, walked calmly over them, crushing men and guns.

Pushing forward, this Martian reached St. George's Hill, where better-trained and braver artillerymen aimed and fired from 1,000 yards away. The shells flashed all around him, and one of his tripod legs was smashed. He uttered a strange howling cry, staggered, and went down. Immediately, the other Martian Fighting-Machines appeared over the trees and aimed their Heat-Rays at the battery. Ammunition exploded; pine trees burst into flames; and only one or two men could be seen escaping down the hill.

The three Fighting-Machines then got together and remained absolutely still for the next half-hour. The small brown creature inside the damaged Fighting-Machine struggled

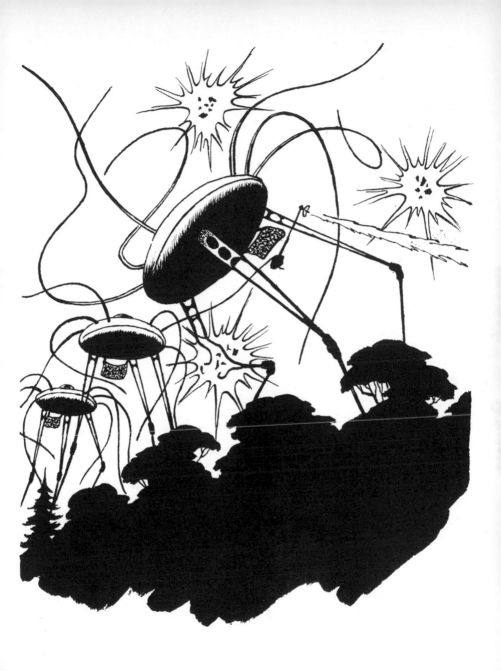

Artillery Shells Hit a Fighting Machine.

out of the hood and immediately began to repair the broken metal.

In a while, he was finished, and the Fighting-Machine was standing erect again. Eight other Fighting-Machines, each carrying several thick black tubes then joined those three. They divided among themselves, then advanced and placed themselves at equal distances along a curve twelve miles long.

As the curate and I were hurrying wearily and painfully along the road, we saw two of them moving across the field towards us. The curate uttered a cry, then began running.

"It's no good running from a Martian," I called after him. "Come, follow me into the ditch. The hedge will cover us."

Seeing the wisdom of my hiding place, he crawled in beside me. The two Martians stopped near us and took up their positions in the curve. Hidden batteries in the woods were waiting silently for their approach.

Peering through the hedge, we heard the distant burst of gunfire. Then another, nearer.

The Martian Repairs His Fighting Machine.

The Martian closest to us raised his black tube high and discharged it like a gun towards the nearby village of Sunbury. The force of the blast made the ground around me tremble. But there was no flash, no smoke, only that explosive noise. The Martian farther along in the curve then discharged a blast also.

I was so excited by these strange guns that I forgot my personal safety and my scalded hands, and I clambered up out of the ditch to see what purpose these guns had. As I did so, another explosive burst followed, and this time it shot something out towards Sunbury. I expected to see smoke or fire, but nothing happened. One minute ... two minutes. ...

A distant tumult of shouting began, then suddenly stopped. Every moment I expected some artillery fire or even an explosion from whatever the Martians had shot into the town. But there was nothing.

The curate and I climbed a hill to get a better look at Sunbury. Hiding in a deserted house, we looked down at the village from an

Excited by Strange Guns

upper window. In the distance we saw several cone-shaped hills suddenly appear out of nowhere. As we stared, the hills grew lower and wider. Then more appeared, and we realized that each time the Martians had discharged a burst from their gunlike black tubes, they had shot out a canister.

These canisters smashed on striking the ground and immediately released a huge volume of black gas which rose in huge hill-like clouds, then spread out and sank over the surrounding country in the form of smoke. The slightest inhaling of that Black Smoke—a kind of poison gas—brought instant death to all who breathed it!

Men and horses near the Black Smoke ran shrieking, falling headlong, shouting with dismay. Guns were suddenly abandoned, their artillerymen choking and writhing on the ground.

The Black Smoke clung so closely to the ground that the only people who were able to

Black Smoke and Instant Death!

escape its deadly poison were those who sought refuge on roofs or in tall trees. When the smoke had served the Martians' purpose, they cleared the air of it by shooting a jet of steam into it.

From the window of the deserted house, the curate and I watched the Martians spreading this strange poison gas over the countryside as they advanced in a direct path to London.

Never once, after the Martian at St. George's Hill was wounded, did they give the artillerymen a ghost of a chance against them. Wherever there was even a possibility of guns hidden in their path, a fresh burst of Black Smoke was discharged. And where the guns were actually in their view, they openly used the Heat-Ray.

Before dawn, the Black Smoke was pouring through the streets of Richmond, just outside London, and the government ordered an immediate evacuation of the great city!

Orders to Evacuate London

Panic at the Railway Station

# CHAPTER 10

## A Terrible Stampede

As Monday dawned, a roaring wave of fear swept through London. There was panic at the railway stations, at the docks along the Thames, and along every road leading north and east out of the city.

By noon, both the railways and the police were completely disorganized. By two o'clock, people were fighting savagely for standing room in the carriages. By three, people were being trampled and crushed in the streets outside the railway stations. Revolvers were fired, people were stabbed, and policemen who

had been trying to direct traffic were so exhausted and enraged that they were fighting
with the very people they were called out to
protect.

As the day wore on, engineers and coal shov-
elers on the trains refused to return to London
with their empty trains to evacuate more of
the fleeing population. People then headed for
the northward roads in ever thickening
crowds.

My brother Frank had tried in vain to get
aboard a northbound train at the Chalk Farm
station.

The engines were plowing through crowds of
shrieking people, and a dozen brave men tried
to keep the crowd from crushing the engineer
against his furnace. So Frank set out on foot,
dodging all sorts of vehicles.

As he trudged through village after village,
he found shops half-opened in the main streets
and people crowding the pavement, doorways,
and windows, staring in astonishment at the
extraordinary procession of fugitives from

An Engine Plows Through the Crowds.

London. Most were on bicycles, but soon there were motor cars, hansom cabs, and carriages hurrying along the road.

"Push on!" was the cry of the fugitives. "Push on! They're coming!"

Some of the people in the carts whipped their horses and quarreled with other drivers; some sat motionless, staring miserably at nothing; some bit at their hands or lay outstretched in the bottom of their wagons. The horses' bits were covered with foam from their mouths, and their eyes were bloodshot.

Trampling past Frank were well-dressed but sad, haggard men and women with stumbling, crying children, their lips black and cracked, their dainty clothes covered with dust, their weary faces smeared with tears. Fighting side by side with them for space in the road were weary, wide-eyed, loud-voiced street urchins in faded black rags.

Wounded soldiers struggled along with workmen in every type of dress. They were all thirsty, weary, and foot-sore. But despite the

"Push On!"

variety in the crowd, there was one thing that they all had in common—the fear and pain on their faces.

"Make way! Make way! The Martians are coming!" rang the hoarse, weak voices in the crowd.

Frank noticed a bearded, eagle-faced man walking near him and dragging a small bag. Suddenly the bag split open, and out poured a mass of gold coins. They rolled in every direction, under the pounding feet of men and horses. The man stopped and looked at the pile of coins, dumbfounded, frozen to the spot. At the moment he froze, the edge of a carriage struck his shoulder and sent him reeling to the side of the road.

As soon as the carriage had passed, he flung himself with both hands open on the heap of coins and began stuffing handfuls in his pockets. At that moment, a horse came riding down on him, and the man fell under the animal's trampling hooves.

"Stop!" screamed my brother as he tried to

Stuffing Handfuls of Coins in His Pockets

grab the horse's bit. But before he could get hold of it, he heard a scream under the wheels and saw the rim pass over the man's back.

Frank bent down to help the wounded man and saw that his back was broken and his legs were unmoving.

"Help me get him out of the road," Frank called to an approaching horseman.

Clutching the wounded man by his jacket, the two men dragged him off the road. All the while the man's wildly grasping hands were trying to gather in his gold.

Suddenly an oncoming carriage crashed into a cart, and the cart and its horse fell towards the three men. The cart and horse missed Frank by a hair, but fell directly on the man with the gold, crushing him to death under the still-spinning wheels.

Frank turned back to the road and was swept along in the noise and confusion for several hours, until several forks in the road appeared, relieving the press of the crowd. Frank took the eastward fork. He passed trains

Dragging the Wounded Man off the Road

headed north, swarming with people, but without signals. He passed multitudes of people drinking at streams, with others pushing and fighting to get near the water.

Towards evening, as hunger and cold began to come on, Frank began to feel utterly exhausted, but he didn't dare sleep. He stopped to rest, however, only to see people hurrying along the road, fleeing from unknown dangers, but going in the direction from which he had just come.

Never before in the history of the world had such a mass of human beings moved and suffered together, as did those fleeing from London. And it wasn't an orderly flight—it was a gigantic and terrible stampede! Six million people, without arms, without food and supplies, were driving headlong without a goal or destination!

Pushing To Get Near the Water

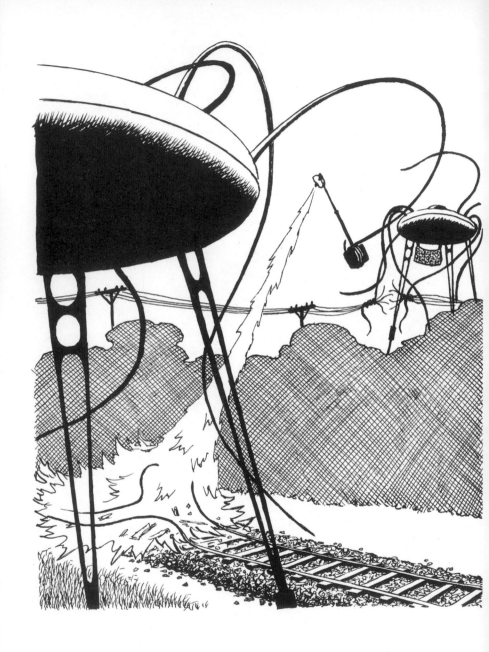

Wrecking Railway and Telegraph Lines

# CHAPTER 11

## The Martians Reach London

The Martians were going to and fro, calmly and methodically spreading their poisonous Black Smoke over every which part of the country and taking possession of it as conquerors. They exploded stores of gun powder, cut every telegraph line, and wrecked those railways they passed. They seemed in no hurry, confident that they were succeeding in demoralizing their enemies and destroying any opposition.

They reached the central part of London Tuesday, suffocating with their Black Smoke the many citizens who had remained behind, stubbornly refusing to leave their houses.

Until noon, the Thames River at London was an astonishing scene. Steamboats and shipping of all sorts anchored in the river were boarded by fugitives seeking escape. Some rowed out; others swam, many drowning in the process.

About one o'clock in the afternoon, a cloud of Black Smoke appeared between the arches of Blackfriars Bridge. At that point, the river became a scene of mad confusion, fighting, and collision. Multitudes of boats and barges jammed under the Tower Bridge, and sailors had to fight savagely against the people who swarmed upon their boats from the piers of the bridge above.

At two o'clock, a Martian appeared beyond the Clock Tower and waded down the river, leaving wreckage along both shores.

Swarming Aboard Boats in the Thames

Boats off the Coast

# CHAPTER 12

## A Warship Attacks the Martians

After several days of walking, with little rest, Frank finally reached the sea near Tillingham. Ships that could no longer come up the Thames sat off the coast—fishing ships from neighboring countries, steam launches, yachts, electric boats, merchant ships, passenger boats, and oil tankers.

A couple of miles out lay an ironclad warship, the *Thunder Child*. Beyond it, in a line, hovered other warships of the British fleet, steamed up and ready for action, yet powerless to stop the Martian conquest.

Frank made his way down to the beach and attracted the attention of some men on a paddle steamer. They sent a boat ashore and demanded 12 pounds to take Frank to Ostend, Belgium. My brother paid the fare, and the seamen rowed him out to the steamer. He bought some food aboard at exorbitant prices and managed to find a seat on deck.

The captain waited until five o'clock that afternoon, picking up passengers until the decks were dangerously crowded. He probably would have waited longer, but at that time, the sound of guns was heard from the South, and it continued to grow louder and louder. Soon Frank saw a column of smoke rising from the land in the distance, and three of the warships were steaming towards it.

The little steamer was heading eastward, away from the crowd of ships along the coast, when a Martian Fighting-Machine appeared, coming up the muddy coast. Seeing this, the steamer's captain cursed himself angrily and

Frank Is Rowed to the Steamer

fearfully for delaying his departure this long. Everyone aboard stood at the rails, staring at that distant shape—higher than the trees and church towers, advancing leisurely like a man out for a stroll.

It was the first Martian my brother had seen, and he stood more amazed than terrified, watching it advance towards the ships, wading farther and farther out into the sea. Soon another Martian appeared and another, striding over trampled trees. They were all stalking toward the sea as if to prevent the escape of the vessels that lay there.

The little steamer's engines throbbed, and her paddlewheels poured out foam behind her, but she moved with terrifying slowness.

Frank looked at the crowd of ships, one passing another, whistling, sending up volumes of steam, letting out sails in their terrified flight. He was so fascinated with this sight and with the approaching Martians that he saw nothing at sea. Suddenly, the steamboat turned sharply to avoid being run down,

The Martians Stalk Towards the Sea.

and Frank was thrown to the deck.

Cheers and shouts went up around him. He sprang to his feet and saw to the starboard a huge iron bulk tearing through the water, tossing huge waves of foam against the steamer. When the spray cleared from his eyes, Frank recognized the torpedo warship, *Thunder Child,* steaming to rescue the threatened ships.

Frank clutched the rails and looked beyond the charged warship at the Martians. Three of the Fighting-Machines were close together and standing so far out to sea that their tripod legs were almost entirely submerged. Sunken like this, they didn't appear as threatening as did the huge iron warship heading their way.

The *Thunder Child* fired no gun, but simply drove full speed towards them. The Martians seemed to regard this new enemy with astonishment, not knowing what to make of it.

Suddenly the lead Martian lowered his black tube and discharged a canister at the warship. It hit her side and bounced off into

A Warship Steams to the Rescue.

the sea, unfolding a torrent of Black Smoke, from which the warship sped away.

The Martians then separated and headed for the shore. One of them raised his Heat-Ray and pointed it at an angle downward. Immediately, a burst of steam rose from the water at its touch. The Heat-Ray must have driven through the iron warship's sides as if they were paper.

Then a flicker of flame rose through the steam, and the Martian instantly reeled and staggered. In a moment he was cut down. The guns of the *Thunder Child* sounded through the air, one after the other.

At the sight of the Martian's collapse, the captain and the passengers on the steamer shouted and yelled. Surging out through the white steam and foam drove the long black warship, flames pouring out of her. She was still alive; her engines still working. She headed straight for the second Martian Fighting-Machine and was within 100 yards of it when

Aflame, but Still Alive!

the Heat-Ray struck. Then, with a violent thud and a blinding flash, her decks and funnels leaped out of the water in a violent explosion. Her flaming wreckage, still driving forward, struck the Fighting-Machine and crumpled it up like a cardboard toy.

"Two!" shouted the captain.

"Two!" echoed everyone at the rails.

The steam on the water hid the third Martian for several minutes. When it cleared, nothing of the *Thunder Child* could be seen, nor was the third Martian Fighting-Machine in sight.

The steamer continued on her way seaward, with other refugee boats and ships doing the same. Frank stood at the rails watching the coast grow faint as the sun sank into evening.

Suddenly, something flat and wide swept across the sky along the coast, and moments later darkness was raining down on the land—it was the Black Smoke!

Collision!

Steam Breaks Up the Black Smoke.

# CHAPTER 13

## Imprisoned at a Martian Pit

While my brother was living through these terrors, the curate and I had been hiding in the deserted house on the hill in Sunbury. We hoped that by staying high on the hill, we could escape the Black Smoke that had fallen on the village below us. We stayed there all Sunday night and all Monday—the day of the panic in London. We were cut off by the Black Smoke from the rest of the world.

On Monday, a Martian came across the field, jetting out steam to break up the Black

Smoke. The steam hissed against the walls of the houses in the village and smashed all the windows it touched.

We waited several hours, then looked out. "The Black Smoke is gone!" I cried. "We're no longer trapped! Let us be off and on our way."

I began gathering food and drink to take along, and covered my burns with some oil and rags I found in the house. I picked up a flannel shirt from one of the closets, and at about five o'clock, we started out along the blackened road to Sunbury.

All along the road were overturned carts and luggage, and dead bodies—horses as well as men—lying twisted at every angle. Everything was covered with a thick layer of black dust.

We saw nothing alive for several hours until we were close to the village of Kew. There, suddenly before us, were a number of people running wildly across a meadow. Over the tree tops, not a hundred yards behind them, was a Martian Fighting-Machine.

It was evident that this Martian was after

Preparing To Be on Their Way

them. In three steps, he was among them, and the people scattered under his feet in all directions. The Martian did not use his Heat-Ray, but simply picked them up, one by one, and tossed them into the large metal basket which hung behind him.

For the first time I realized that perhaps the Martians had some other purpose for human beings than to destroy them. The curate and I stood for a moment, terrified, then turned and jumped into a ditch. We lay there, scarcely daring to whisper to each other until late that night.

It was nearly eleven o'clock before we gathered enough courage to start again. After several hours of sneaking in and out of bushes along the road, we reached a deserted house near Mortlake. There, we discovered a store of food—two loaves of bread, an uncooked steak, half a ham, several bottles of beer, two bags of beans, tins of soup, fish, and biscuits, and a dozen bottles of wine. I describe these so carefully, for the curate and I were to exist on this

The Martians Capture Human Beings.

food for the next two weeks.

We sat down immediately in the kitchen in the dark—for we dared not light a lamp—and had bread and ham and a bottle of beer.

"Hurry, let us be on our way," urged the frightened curate.

"We must keep up our strength by eating," I replied.

And then it happened—the thing that was to imprison us. As we sat in the dark kitchen, everything in the room suddenly became visible in a blinding glare of green light. This was followed by a concussion such as I have never heard before or since. Moments later came a crash of glass, the rattle of falling walls, and the tumbling of plaster ceilings.

I was knocked headlong across the floor and against the oven. I lay unconscious for a long time, the curate told me afterward, as he dabbed water over me. My temple was pounding from a bruise, but I sat up.

"Don't move," said the curate. "The floor is covered with broken dishes. You can't move a

Ceilings and Walls Crash Down!

step without making noise, and I believe they are outside."

We both sat quite still. Outside, very near, I heard a metallic rattle.

"A Martian," said the curate.

Our situation was so strange that for three or four hours we scarcely moved. And then daylight entered, not through the window which was black, but through a triangular hole which had been made in a brick wall behind us. With this light, we saw the inside of the kitchen for the first time.

Smashed dishes and glassware and clumps of soil and rocks lay at our feet. Outside, the soil was piled high against the kitchen wall, blocking all window openings. The rest of the house's walls seemed to have collapsed, with only the kitchen's walls still standing—but where...and under what?

As the sun rose and streamed in through the triangular hole in the wall, we peeked out and saw the shiny brown body of a Martian standing guard over a gleaming cylinder.

Imprisoned in the Kitchen!

"The fifth cylinder!" I whispered. "The fifth shot from Mars has hit this house and buried us under the ruins!"

"God have mercy on us," whispered the curate, and he immediately began sobbing.

We made our way softly out of the kitchen and into the dark scullery—the small room off the kitchen where dishes are washed and vegetables cleaned. We lay there quite still, scarcely daring to breathe. I kept my eyes fixed on the kitchen with its faint light.

We sat crouched in the scullery, silent and shivering for hours, until weariness closed our eyes. We probably spent nearly a whole day asleep, but when I awoke, I heard a metallic hammering outside, and the curate was gone!

"Curate? Curate?" I whispered, but received no reply.

I felt my way to the door leading to the kitchen and saw the curate across the room lying against the triangular hole that looked out on the Martians. It was still daylight, I saw through the hole, but evening was coming

"The Fifth Cylinder!"

on. I carefully crawled towards the curate, avoiding all the broken dishes littering the floor.

When I raised myself to look out, I saw that the quiet country road that had been there yesterday was gone. In its place was a deep hole vastly larger than the pit the Martians had made at Woking. The cylinder lay in it now, with the earth that once filled that hole "splashed" in high piles at the top.

The front of the house we were in had been destroyed, but, by chance, the kitchen and scullery had escaped. They now stood buried under tons on earth on every side, except the side facing the cylinder in the pit.

On the far edge of the pit, amid the smashed shrubs, one of the great Fighting-Machines stood stiff and tall against the evening sky. Inside the pit strange creatures were crawling slowly and painfully out of the cylinder, panting for breath, stirring weakened tentacles, and moving feebly after their vast journey across space.

Wells Crawls Toward the Curate.

Nearby was a complicated, glittering machine busy at work. It was a sort of metallic crab with five jointed legs, an extraordinary number of levers and bars, and long, clutching tentacles around its body. Three of these tentacles were fishing out metal rods, plates, and bars from the cylinder, and depositing them on a flat surface of earth behind it.

A Martian seemed to be controlling the tentacles' movements from a position at the crab's head, while other Martians, not in machines, worked around the pit. For the first time I was able to study these creatures up close, without danger of being seen.

The Martians were the most unearthly creatures imaginable. They were huge round bodies—or rather—huge round heads—about four feet in diameter. Each body had a face in front of it. This face had a pair of dark-colored eyes, and just beneath them, a kind of fleshy beak. The face had no nostrils—indeed, the Martian seemed not to have any sense of smell. In back

A Metallic Crab at Work

of his head, or body—I hardly know what to call it—was a thin, single round drum covered with a filmy skin. This was later discovered to be an ear, though it must have been almost useless in our dense air.

Around his mouth were sixteen thin, whip-like tentacles, arranged in two groups of eight each, which he used like hands.

Scientists later discovered that the largest part of the creature was his brain, which sent enormous nerves to his eyes, ear, and tentacles. Bulky lungs led to his mouth, and the convulsions of his outer skin were caused by his breathing in the dense air on earth. This, then, was all of the Martian's body. Aside from a brain and lungs, the Martians had no other inner organs.

There were four other ways in which the Martians' bodies differed from ours. First, their bodies did not sleep, but worked continuously, just as the heart of a man does. Second, the Martians had no male or female differences. A young Martian is born by budding

The Most Unearthly Creature Imaginable!

off its parent, just as certain bulbs in our plant life do. Third, the Martian's body, which probably descended gradually from beings much like humans, developed only into a brain and hands (the two bunches of tentacles), while the rest of the body disappeared from lack of use. Last, tiny organisms which cause hundreds of diseases such as fevers, tumors, and cancers on Earth have either never existed on Mars, or were destroyed by Martian science years ago.

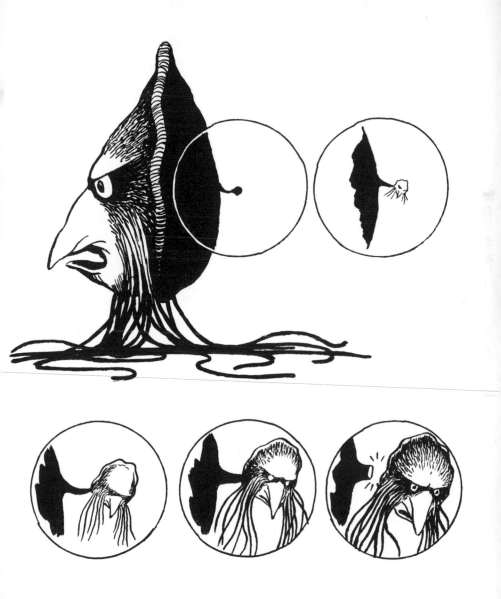

The Birth of a Martian

The Curate Refuses to Conserve Food.

# CHAPTER 14

## A Terrible Human Yell

As the days wore on, the curate's endless, helpless complaining was driving me nearly crazy. He would weep for hours, while I sat in the darkness trying to think out a plan of escape. He ate and drank much more than I did, and refused to listen to my pleas and threats that we conserve our food, for as I saw it, our only chance to save ourselves was to stay in the house until the Martians were finished in the pit.

The curate was at the peephole, and I was

sitting below him when he made a sudden movement backward and came sliding down beside me in the darkness, grasping my arm in terror. My curiosity gave me courage, and I looked out.

The pit was lit by a flickering green flame that came from one of the machines working near the cylinder. Several Martians were standing in front of a mound of blue-green powder, and a Fighting-Machine, its legs folded and shortened, stood in one corner. As I crouched, studying this Fighting-Machine, I realized that its hood did, indeed, contain a Martian. As the green flames rose, I could see the oily gleam of his skin and the brightness of his eyes.

Suddenly I heard a yell—a human yell, and a long tentacle reached over the shoulder of the machine to the little basket hanging on its back. Then something—something struggling violently—was lifted high against the twilight sky. It was a man—a stout, well-dressed, middle-aged man. He was clutched in one of the

A Martian Prisoner!

steely tentacles of the Fighting-Machine as it swung him through the air.

The next minute, the tentacle lowered him to the ground in front of the group of Martians, who immediately surrounded him. For a moment there was silence. Then I heard a long, horrible human shriek, followed by the cheerful hooting of the Martians. I suddenly realized, to my horror, that these Martians nourished themselves by taking the fresh blood of living creatures and injecting it into their veins through a little pipe!

I fell away from the slit, covered my ears with my hands, and ran for the scullery. The curate and I crouched there all night, caught up in the horror and fascination of what we had seen. I tried desperately for hours to think of a way to escape, but found none.

By the next day, the curate could no longer speak. Seeing the Martians' horrible atrocity had robbed him of all his reason, and he behaved like an animal. I knew I must not let that happen to me too.

The Martians Surround Their Victim.

The Curate Tries To Push Wells Away.

# CHAPTER 15

## The Death of the Curate

By the sixth day of our imprisonment, nothing had changed. I was at the peephole, and usually the curate was beside me, trying to push me away. Suddenly I looked around.... I was alone. I was struck with a sudden, alarming thought, and I went quickly and quietly back into the scullery. In the darkness, I heard the curate drinking.

I grabbed the bottle of wine away from him and as we struggled, it struck the floor and broke. As we stood panting, I gasped, "From this moment on, I am dividing the food in the pantry into rations to last us ten days. You will not eat any more today!"

For two days his complaining and our wrestling contests continued. At times I teased him, persuaded him, and even bribed him to bear up; other times I had to beat and kick him madly to stop his hysterics. But neither kindness nor force succeeded. He continued his attacks on the food and his noisy babbling to himself. Slowly I began to realize that my only companion in this sickly darkness was an insane man!

On the eighth day, the curate began to talk wildly and loudly instead of whispering. "We have sinned!" he cried. "Sinned! We must be punished! I shall bring the Martians down to punish us!"

"Be still!" I begged, rising to my feet in terror. "For God's sake...."

"No!" shouted the curate at the top of his lungs, flinging his arms up to the heavens. "I

"I Must Be Punished!"

must be punished before it is too late! I must go!"

With that, he turned and lunged for the door leading to the kitchen. I reached for a meat chopper hanging on the wall and went after him. Just as he was opening the kitchen door, I reached him, but couldn't bear using the blade on him, so I struck him with the butt end of the chopper. He fell forward into the kitchen and lay stretched on the ground.

As I leaned against the door, trying to catch my breath, I suddenly heard a noise. One of the gripping tentacles of the crablike Handling-Machine had pushed in through the peephole and was now feeling its way over the fallen beams and broken dishes. I stood terrified, staring at the large dark eyes of the Martian that suddenly appeared at the peephole atop his Handling-Machine. As I stared, I forced myself back against the scullery door, stumbling over the curate on the way.

The tentacle was now two or three yards into the room, twisting and turning with

A Martian Appears at the Peephole.

strange, sudden movements. For several moments, I stood fascinated by its slow, determined advance. Then, trembling violently, I lunged for the door to the coal cellar, a few steps farther away, and stepped inside. Had the Martian seen me? What was it doing now?

In the darkness of the coal cellar I heard the tentacle moving very quietly in the kitchen. Every now and then it tapped against the wall with a slight metallic ring. Then I heard a heavy body—I knew too well what it was— being dragged across the kitchen floor towards the opening.

My curiosity couldn't resist, so I opened the door slightly and peeped into the kitchen. With the bright sunlight streaming through the peephole, I saw the Martian in his Handling-Machine outside studying the curate's head. I feared he would realize that I was near from the mark of the blow on the curate's head, so I quietly closed the door and crept back to the coal cellar. There, in the darkness, I covered myself as quickly and as much as I could

A Body Is Dragged Towards the Opening.

with the firewood and coal piled in the bins.

Then the metallic jingle began again, slowly following a path all over the kitchen. When it scraped across the cellar door, I held my breath for what seemed to be an endless few minutes. Then I heard it fumbling at the latch! The Martians understood doors!

It worked at the latch for a few minutes, and then the door opened. In the darkness all I could see was something like an elephant's trunk waving towards me, touching and examining the wall, the ceiling, the coal, and the wood.

Then it touched the heel of my boot. I was on the verge of screaming, but I bit down hard on my hand to muffle my scream. For a while, the tentacle was silent, then with a sudden click, it gripped something. I mentally checked every part of my body for a cold metallic touch . . . but nothing. The tentacle had probably taken a lump of coal to examine as it went out of the cellar.

I listened, whispering tearful prayers for my

The Tentacle Touches Wells's Boot.

safety. Then I heard the slow, deliberate sound creeping towards me again, scratching against the walls and tapping the furniture as it approached the cellar door. But it went instead into the pantry, and I heard the rattling of biscuit tins and the smashing of bottles. And then there was silence! Had it gone? . . .

I waited in suspense in the darkness all during the tenth day, buried among the coals and the firewood, not even daring to crawl out for the drink I craved.

Examining the Pantry

Every Scrap of Food Is Gone!

# CHAPTER 16

## Escape!

It wasn't until the next day, the eleventh, that I felt safe enough to venture out from the coal cellar. I checked the pantry, but it was empty; every scrap of food was gone! Apparently, the Martian had taken it all on the previous day. At this discovery, I began to lose hope for the first time.

So, on the eleventh and twelfth days I had no food or water. At first, my mouth and throat were parched, and my strength slowly began to leave me. I sat in the darkness of the scullery, wretched and despondent, thinking only of eating.

By the end of the twelfth day, my throat was so painful that I decided to risk alerting the Martians just so I could use the creaking water pump at the kitchen sink. The couple of glassfuls of blackened rain water greatly refreshed me, and the fact that no prying tentacle followed the noise of my pumping greatly relieved me.

All during the thirteenth and fourteenth days I dozed, but my sleep was filled with horrible dreams, sometimes of the curate's death, sometimes of sumptuous dinners.

Early on the fifteenth day I heard the curious, familiar sound of a dog's scratching coming from the kitchen. Creeping out of the coal cellar, I saw a dog's nose sniffing in at the peephole. Smelling me, he began to bark.

"Here, boy," I whispered, hoping to lure him inside where he wouldn't attract the attention of the Martians. "Good dog."

But then he suddenly withdrew his head

"Here, Boy."

and disappeared. I listened for several minutes, but the pit was still. Finally, I dared a look.

In one corner of the pit, a group of black crows were fighting over the skeletons of the dead bodies the Martians had eaten. But there was not another living thing in the pit. I stared hard, scarcely believing my eyes. All the machinery was gone, and only the empty circular pit remained.

Slowly, I pushed myself out through the peephole and stood upon the mound of rubble. Not a sign of Martians to be seen. My chance of escape had come!

Trembling violently, I scrambled to the top of the house in which I had been buried for so long. I looked around again—north, south, east, west—not a Martian was visible.

When I had last seen this part of the village of Mortlake, it had been a street of comfortable white houses surrounded by rich shady trees. Now, as I stood on a mound of ruined bricks and gravel, all I saw were burned, dead trees

Crows Fight Over a Skeleton.

and wrecked houses.

But a gentle breeze blew, and I took long, hard tastes of that rich, sweet air! Once my lungs tasted the air, my stomach reminded me of my long and dismal fast. I looked around for someplace to obtain food. Beyond a low wall I saw a garden patch, and I hurried towards it.

Here I found some young onions and carrots and a few gladiolus bulbs. I gobbled them up, then climbed back over the wall and made my way towards the next village.

Farther along the way, I happened upon a group of mushrooms, which I devoured, then I drank from the brown flowing water of a shallow stream.

I rested for the remainder of the daylight in some thick shrubbery. My weakened condition would not permit me to push on.

After sunset, I struggled on along the road towards the village of Putney. From a hill outside the village, I looked down on blackened trees, blackened, desolate ruins, and silence.

Blackened Ruins from the Heat-Ray

The Heat-Ray had passed here. As I gazed down at the silent desolation, I felt that mankind had been swept out of existence, that I was the last man left alive, and that the Martians had gone on to seek food elsewhere. Perhaps, even now, they were destroying Berlin or Paris, or were heading for America.

I found a deserted inn on top of Putney Hill. I broke into it and ransacked every room for food. I turned up a crust of bread, already gnawed on by rats, two cans of pineapple, and several hard biscuits.

Before going to bed—my first real bed since I left my home at Maybury—I prowled from window to window, peering out for some sign of the monsters. As I lay in bed, reinforced by some of the food I had found, I turned my thoughts to the problem of the Martians and the fate of my wife. I had no information on either, but I could imagine a hundred things. As I started doing this, the night became terrible. I found myself sitting up in bed, staring at the dark, and praying that if my wife had died in

Wells Finds Food at a Deserted Inn.

this war, that her death would have been quick, with a blast of the Heat-Ray, rather than have her fall victim to the Martians' search for human blood.

The morning was bright and fine as I crept out of the inn and started down the road. My plan was to go on to Leatherhead, though I knew I had very little chance of finding my wife there. If she wasn't dead, then surely she and her cousins would have fled. Perhaps I could learn where. My heart ached to find her.

I had stopped to look at a swarm of little frogs frolicking in a swamp in the morning sunshine, when suddenly, I had the odd feeling of being watched. I spun around and saw something crouching in a clump of bushes.

As I walked slowly towards it, it rose . . . and became a man armed with a cutlass. He stood silent and motionless, staring at me.

He was dressed in clothes as dusty and filthy as my own. His black hair fell over his eyes, and his face was dark and dirty and sunken, with a large red cut across his chin.

An Armed Man in the Swamp!

"Stop!" he cried hoarsely, when I was a few feet from him. "Where do you come from?"

"I come from Maybury Hill," I said. "I was on my way to Leatherhead when I was buried near a pit the Martians made around one of their cylinders. But I worked my way out."

"Well, you can't stay here," he said. "This is my country. There is only food for one."

"I don't wish to stay here," I answered slowly. "I have been buried in the ruins of a house for thirteen or fourteen days. I don't know what has happened. I only know I want to go to Leatherhead to search for my wife."

The man looked at me doubtfully, then suddenly shot out a pointing finger. "It is you!" he cried. "The man who took me in and fed me. I thought you were killed at Weybridge."

I recognized him at the same moment. "You are the artilleryman who came to my home."

"We are lucky ones!" he said, shaking my hand. "After the Martians left the river, I escaped across the fields. That was sixteen days ago, and . . . Good Lord, man, your hair has

"It Is You!"

turned gray! . . . But we are out too much in the open. Let us crawl under those bushes and talk."

"Have you seen any Martians?" I asked, once we were safely hidden.

"They've gone towards London," he replied. "At night, the sky is lit up with them moving. And just last night they had something up in the air. I believe they've built a Flying-Machine and are learning to fly."

"Fly!" I cried. "Then it is all over for us. If they can fly, they will simply go around the world and destroy all life."

He nodded and said sadly, "It is all over for us already. We're down; we're beat. They've lost one—just one. But they've walked all over us and crippled the greatest power in the world!"

I still held out a vague hope, but the artilleryman went on, dashing that hope.

"The death of that Martian in the river at Weybridge was an accident. Besides, these are only pioneers. They'll keep on coming. I've

They've Built a Flying Machine."

seen those green stars, and they're probably still falling somewhere every night."

Suddenly I recalled the night at Ogilvy's observatory, and I explained to the artilleryman, "After the tenth shot, they fired no more."

"Probably just something wrong with their gun," he said. "They'll get it right again. Nothing will change the end. It's just like men and ants, and that's what we are now to the Martians, just like ants only . . . we're eatable ants! First they'll smash us up—our shops, our guns, our railways, our cities. Then they'll begin catching us as they want us, picking out the best and storing us in cages. Our cities, our nations, our civilization, our progress—it's all over. We're beat."

"But if that is so, what is there to live for?"

"Thinking men like me are going on living," he replied. "I don't intend to be caught and tamed and fattened by those brown creepers. I've thought it all out. There's food all around here—canned goods in shops, wines, mineral waters. The only chance we've got, as I see it,

"After the Tenth Shot, They Fired No More."

is to keep ourselves alive and learn—learn as much about them as we can."

I was shocked, yet impressed by the man's determination. "Great God!" I cried. "You are a man, indeed! But go on."

"Those of us who'll escape the Martians must invent a sort of life where we can live in safety. No weak or useless ones will be allowed to join us. We can live underground, in the miles and miles of drains and railway tunnels below the streets of London."

"It's living like wild, savage rats!" I cried.

"But we're saving ourselves and we're learning—learning to operate those Fighting-Machines and those Heat-Rays. Knowing that, man can regain his power on earth."

We talked for a long while that morning, crouched in the bushes. Then, after scanning the sky for Martians, we hurried to the house on Putney Hill where the artilleryman had his hideout.

We feasted on cans of turtle soup and wine, which he had found in the pantry. All the while

The Artilleryman Describes an Escape.

we ate and drank, the artilleryman continued to talk of his grand plans to capture a Fighting-Machine. When it turned dark, I went up on the roof to gaze out across the valley towards London.

I stayed on the roof a long time, gazing out at the darkened city and feeling like a traitor to my wife and to all mankind for having eaten and drunk, while the rest of my countrymen were suffering and dying. I made up my mind then—I would leave the artilleryman to his dreams, his drink, and his food, and go on into London. There, I would have the best chance of learning what the Martians and my fellow men were doing.

Sharing a Feast and Making Plans

Hurrying Past Dead Bodies

# CHAPTER 17

## The Martians' Destruction

I left the artilleryman and made my way down Putney Hill. Black dust covered the roadway as I approached the town of Fulham. The streets were horribly quiet and the shops broken into. I found food—sour, hard, and moldy, but eatable—in a baker's shop. I hurried past dead bodies in the streets. The black powder covered them, but the smells told me they had been dead for many days!

I proceeded towards the outskirts of London, where the streets were clear of dead bodies and black powder. It was here that I first heard the howling. It sounded like sobbing notes, *"Ulla, ulla, ulla, ulla."* As I headed north, the howling seemed to grow louder.

*"Ulla, ulla, ulla, ulla,"* cried the voice.

The wailing filled me with dread. "Why am I wandering alone in the city of the dead?" I asked myself. I felt intolerably lonely.

I came into London myself through Oxford Street by the Marble Arch. Here again I found black powder and several bodies. I wandered on through the silent streets, past silent houses towards Regents Park. As I entered the park, I saw, far away over the trees, the hood of the Martian Fighting-Machine that the howling was coming from.

Strangely enough, I was not frightened, perhaps because I was too tired. I calmly walked towards him, watching him. He did not move. He appeared to be standing and yelling, but I could not discover the reason for this. The howling of *"Ulla, ulla, ulla, ulla"* confused me, but though I was curious to know the reason

A Fighting Machine in Regents Park

for it, I was still afraid of it.

I turned back away from the park and ran along the street, hidden by the terraces of the ruined houses. As I ran, I heard a chorus of barks and saw a dog with a piece of decaying red meat in his jaws coming towards me. He was being chased by a pack of other starving dogs. They paid no attention to me and continued their yelping down the road. Then the wailing of *"Ulla, ulla, ulla, ulla"* began again.

I came upon a wrecked Fighting-Machine a little farther on. It lay smashed and twisted among the ruins it had made. Its tentacles were bent and its front was shattered. It seemed to have driven blindly into a house and then crashed down along with it. Could the Martian have lost control of his machine?

I clambered to the top of the ruins of a house for a closer look at the Fighting-Machine. In the twilight, I could make out a blood-smeared seat and the gnawed flesh of the Martian's body—flesh which the dogs had left behind.

I left that ghastly sight behind and pushed

Starving Dogs!

on. Far ahead, through a gap in the trees, I saw another Martian, standing motionless in the park near the zoo. I turned and ran until long after midnight, when I found shelter in a cabman's shack.

Before dawn, my courage returned, and I headed once more towards Regents Park. On the top of a hill along the way was another Martian, erect and motionless like the others. For the moment, my mind snapped. I would die and end it, I decided. So I marched on recklessly towards it. As I drew nearer and the light of dawn came up, I saw a multitude of black birds circling around the hood of the motionless monster.

I hurried up the hill, a wild, excited thought flashing through my mind. Did I dare believe it? Out of the hood hung shreds of the Martian's brain, which the hungry birds were pecking and tearing at.

High mounds of earth had been piled at the top of the hill, and as I climbed up one mound and looked down, I saw the final and largest

Black Birds Circle a Motionless Monster.

pit the Martians had made. Scattered around were about fifty Martians—some in their now-rigid Handling-Machines, and some silent and laid in a row—and they were all dead!

Although I couldn't understand at the time what had caused the Martians' death, I later discovered that it was the earth's bacteria, which their bodies couldn't fight. So, after all of man's efforts had failed, the Martians had been destroyed by some of the smallest things God had put on this earth—bacteria!

Since the beginning of time, man has developed the power to resist the diseases caused by these bacteria. But there are no bacteria on Mars, and as soon as the Martians arrived and as soon as they drank and ate, our microscopic germs began their work.

As I stood staring into the pit, my heart lightened. Across the pit on its farthest rim lay the giant Flying-Machine the Martians had been experimenting with when death stopped them. And death had come not a day too soon.

Down the slope of the hill stood the other

Wells Finds the Martians—*All Dead!*

two Martian Fighting-Machines I had seen during the night. They were glittering in the early morning sun, their now harmless tripods—still. The only movement came from the birds tearing the red flesh to shreds.

And all around the pit, as if saved by a miracle from God, stretched the great city of London, silent, abandoned, and in ruins.

"Man might still be alive in these streets," I thought, "and this dead city can once more come to life and be powerful." The joy that swept through me at this idea brought tears to my eyes.

I extended my hands towards the sky. "Thank You, God!" I whispered, weeping. "Thank You for them. But for me, for my wife, and for our old life of hope and love—that has ceased forever."

"Thank You, God!"

Wiring the News to Paris

# CHAPTER 18

## Returning Home

And now comes the strangest part of my story. Everything that had happened to me is clear in my memory...until the moment when I stood on the hill overlooking London, thanking God. And then I forgot. I remember nothing of the next three days.

I later learned that other wanderers like me had discovered the Martians' destruction the night before I did. One man—the first—had managed to reach a telegraph office and wire the news to Paris. The joyful news then flashed all over the world. Thousands of cities, chilled with the fear that they would be the next Martian targets, rang church bells, sent people out into the streets weeping with joy, and began shipping food supplies to London.

But I remember none of this. With my sanity and my memory gone, I wandered the streets of London. On the third day of my wandering, I was taken in by some kindly people who had found me singing, weeping, and raving in the streets. Even though these people had enough problems of their own, they sheltered me and protected me from myself until my mind was back to normal. Then, they very gently broke the news to me that Leatherhead had been destroyed by a Martian and that not a soul had survived.

I was lonely and sad, but the people were patient with me. Soon I began to crave one more look at what remained of my happy past on Maybury Hill. They pleaded with me not to go, but I had to.

So I went out again into the streets. They

Wells's Sanity and Memory Are Gone!

were already busy with returning people. Some shops were even opening. The churches were distributing bread sent across from France. How busy everyone was on that bright sunny day, even though they were still in dirty rags, their yellow faces still sunken.

Free trains were running, taking people to their homes. Here, the first rush was over, and I boarded a train and found a compartment for myself. I sat with folded arms, looking at the blackened ruins that sped past the windows. All along the track, hundreds of workers were re-laying the rails.

I got off at Byfleet station, since Woking was still under repair, and started on the road to Maybury. I passed the spot where the Martian had first appeared to me in the thunderstorm. Here, out of curiosity, I turned aside to find the broken cart I had rented to take my wife to Leatherhead. Next to it lay the whitened bones of the horse, scattered and chewed on. I stood for a while, remembering—

I looked ahead toward my house with a

Boarding a Train for Home

quick flash of hope. But it faded immediately. The door had been broken, and was now opening and closing from the breeze. Curtains fluttered out of my open study window—the window from which the artilleryman and I had watched the pit on Horsell Common nearly four weeks ago.

I stumbled into the hall and up the stairs to my study. On my desk was the article I had been writing on the day of the opening of the first cylinder. It was an article on how civilization would develop in the future.

"In about two hundred years," I had written, "we may expect—" and the sentence had been left unfinished when I had gone to get my newspaper from the delivery boy and had listened to his odd story of "the dead men from Mars."

I went down into the dining room. Meat and bread were on the table, moldy and decayed, and a bottle of beer overturned, just as the artilleryman and I had left them.

My home was desolate. The faint hope I had

Hope Fades

cherished for weeks—the hope of seeing my dear wife again—was gone.

And then a strange thing occurred. I heard a man's voice coming from outside the front door.

"It is no use," said the voice. "The house is deserted. No one has been here all these weeks. Do not stay here and torment yourself. No one has escaped but you."

I was startled! Who knew I was here? Who knew what thoughts were in my head?

I turned and took a step outside the french doors leading from the dining room into the garden. And then, as amazed and afraid as I, stood my cousin . . . and my wife! Her face was white, but she gave a faint cry when she saw me.

"I came," she said. "I knew . . . I knew. . . ." She clutched her throat and swayed.

I rushed forward and caught her in my arms before she fainted.

A Joyous Reunion!

Discovering How the Martians Died

# CHAPTER 19

# The Future of Man

After the war, although the cause of the Martians' deaths was discovered to be Earth's bacteria, no one was able to determine what the Martians' Black Smoke was made of, or how their Heat-Rays worked.

But a question of more serious world-wide interest is the possibility of another attack from Mars. I believe this is a possibility, and we should be prepared. We should keep a constant watch on that part of Mars from which the shots were discharged so as to know when to expect the arrival of the next attack. That way, the cylinder could be destroyed with dynamite or artillery fire before it was cool enough for the Martians to come out.

In any case, we have learned that we cannot regard our planet as a secure home for man.

Perhaps, however, across the immensity of space, the Martians have watched the fate of these pioneers of theirs and have learned a lesson. Perhaps they will try to find a safer settlement on another planet. In fact, several astronomers believe that the Martians have already made a successful landing on Venus.

Man's view of the universe has expanded, too, as a result of the Martians' attack. As my wife and I gaze in the heavens, we realize that if the astronomers are correct and if the Martians have reached Venus, it isn't impossible for man to travel to other planets too. And so, one day when the slow cooling of the sun makes the earth uninhabitable, as it must eventually do, man can continue his life elsewhere in this vast universe.

Realizing That Man Can Travel in Space

B5815